The Poisonwood Bible

Barnes & Noble® Reader's Companion™

Today's take on tomorrow's classics.

FICTION

THE CORRECTIONS by Jonathan Franzen
I KNOW WHY THE CAGED BIRD SINGS by Maya Angelou
THE JOY LUCK CLUB by Amy Tan
THE LOVELY BONES by Alice Sebold
THE POISONWOOD BIBLE by Barbara Kingsolver
THE RED TENT by Anita Diamant
WE WERE THE MULVANEYS by Joyce Carol Oates
WHITE TEETH by Zadie Smith

NONFICTION

THE ART OF WAR by Sun Tzu
A BRIEF HISTORY OF TIME by Stephen Hawking
GUNS, GERMS, AND STEEL by Jared Diamond
JOHN ADAMS by David McCullough

BARBARA KINGSOLVER'S
The Poisonwood Bible

BARNES
&NOBLE
B O O K S

EDITORIAL DIRECTOR Justin Kestler
EXECUTIVE EDITOR Ben Florman
DIRECTOR OF TECHNOLOGY Tammy Hepps

SERIES EDITOR John Crowther
MANAGING EDITOR Vincent Janoski

WRITER Barbara Fisher
EDITOR Matt Blanchard
DESIGN Dan O. Williams, Matt Daniels

This edition published by Spark Publishing

Spark Publishing
A Division of SparkNotes LLC
120 Fifth Avenue, 8th Floor
New York, NY 10011

ISBN 1-58663-859-9

Library of Congress Cataloging-in-Publication Data available upon request

Printed and bound in the United States

Contents

Barnes & Noble® Reader's Companion™

WITH INTELLIGENT CONVERSATION AND ENGAGING commentary from a variety of perspectives, Barnes & Noble Reader's Companions are the perfect complement to today's most widely read and discussed books.

○ ○ ○

Whether you're reading on your own or as part of a book club, Barnes & Noble Reader's Companions provide insights and perspectives on today's most interesting reads: What are other people saying about this book? What's the author trying to tell me?

○ ○ ○

Pick up the Barnes & Noble Reader's Companion to learn more about what you're reading. From the big picture down to the details, you'll get today's take on tomorrow's classics.

The Poisonwood Bible

The Edge of the World

The Poisonwood Bible is a gripping story that weaves one family's struggles with those of an African country in turmoil.

○ ○ ○

NOVELS THAT ILLUMINATE the larger political world are rare in American fiction. Novels that do this *and* create a moving personal story are even rarer. *The Poisonwood Bible* is that rarity. It speaks eloquently about the political situation in the former Belgian Congo during the struggle for independence in the early 1960s. This struggle unfolds through the lens of a wrenching human drama, the fall of the Price family of Bethlehem, Georgia.

We meet the Prices one after another. Each one introduces herself, beginning with Orleanna, the mother. Her four daughters follow: fifteen-year-old Rachel, fourteen-year-old twins Leah and Adah, and the baby, five-year-old Ruth May. They've come to the Congo following their father, Nathan Price, a fierce Baptist missionary preacher, a man utterly secure in the word of his god. It's 1959. Over the course of more than thirty years, Nathan's god will be tested, as will the character, resources, will, and endurance of Nathan's wife and daughters.

At first, the Prices' encounter with Kilanga Village is a humorous series of misunderstandings and missed connections. The Prices come to Africa with all the wrong things—Betty Crocker cake mixes, linen suits, and pinking shears—and all the wrong ideas—Christian baptism, personal property, modesty, cleanliness, and privacy. These misunderstandings are representative of deeper divisions. The girls, each in her own time and way, absorb the culture into which they're unhappily thrust. Orleanna,

1

desperate to keep her children fed, safe, and alive, doesn't have the leisure of looking beyond these immediate and urgent needs. Nathan, secure as the all-knowing, law-enforcing father, doesn't think beyond himself and his faith.

Each girl has her own distinct voice and point of view, each of which shifts over time. Rachel, a vain, self-absorbed, white-blond beauty, is attentive to surfaces—how people look and smell and dress, how the air feels, how food tastes. Leah, an idealist and tomboy, strives to be her father's favorite. Adah, who walks with a limp and barely ever speaks (as a

> # "My father wears his faith like the bronze breastplate of God's foot soldiers, while our mother's is more like a good cloth coat with a secondhand fit."

result of an accident during her difficult birth), plays with words silently and alone. The fearless and friendly Ruth May, on the other hand, joins in with the children of the village.

These varied personalities and approaches to the world complement and contradict one another and create a chorus of relative truth. Altogether, their accounts give us some idea of what is happening, but no one view is sufficient; no single truth emerges. The girls convey a complex world. They tell us about the American South as they tell us about Africa. They tell us about Africa as they tell us about themselves. They tell us about themselves as they pass judgment on one another. Meaning unfolds slowly and haltingly, as the speakers reveal layer upon layer of definition, description and explanation.

Africa and the women of the Price family are engaged in a parallel struggle. Both seek liberation from iron-fisted rule. For Africa, it's the colonialism of white foreign powers. For the Price women, it's Nathan and his omnipotent, omnipresent Jesus. The Congo frees itself briefly under the leadership of Patrice Lumumba but falls back under the control of a Western puppet dictatorship led by Mobutu Sese Soko. Each of the Price girls frees herself from her father in one way or another—some achieving almost complete freedom, some succumbing to different forms of male domination. All suffer, and some die. None remains unchanged.

Nor do we. *The Poisonwood Bible* uncovers a world at once strange and immediate. The Prices, with their unquestioning beliefs—in Christ, in America, in the place of women in society, in the Jim Crow laws of American South—are familiar in their prejudices. Africa is utterly new and strange to them and perhaps to many of us. But as the Prices learn slowly and painfully to see the world differently and to consider other systems of belief, we learn as well.

These are not lessons taught in class, but lived in the flesh, hearts, and souls of characters we come to know and love. Recognition and revelation take time, and Kingsolver paces her story beautifully so that political awareness and personal growth dovetail, each informing the other. Kingsolver balances the postcolonial narrative and the personal family saga with remarkable agility and grace. If some novels widen the doors of perception, this one throws them open.

BOOK ONE: GENESIS
THE THINGS WE CARRIED, KILANGA, 1959

One by one, the characters introduce themselves in their own voices. Orleanna begins from an undetermined point in the distant future, looking back on her family's unbearable stay in Africa. She is now in Sanderling Island, Georgia. She wants to win our sympathy. Moreover, she wants our understanding and forgiveness for the ignorance of her family, as well as for the arrogance and folly of white men. There is no doubt that Orleanna walked away from her personal tragedies with excruciating lessons. This section is laden with a sense of guilt and loss, and inferences to death. We're prepared for the worst. Her tone is elegiac, hurt, and wistful. She tries to imagine different outcomes, different stories. But Orleanna is left with her own tale—a personal and terrible truth

Leah, the whole and healthy twin, is next to come forward. In her adolescent voice she describes the members of the family, how they prepared for the journey to Africa, how they carried their excessive and inappropriate baggage. She provides us with more information than she realizes.

Baby Ruth May's childish point of view is perfectly suited to reporting prejudice and ignorance. She tells us with certainty that the black people of Africa are the descendants of Ham, cursed to be slaves. Back home in Georgia, there are "Jimmy Crow laws" that keep these dark people out of the restaurants and that identify Thursday as their day to go to the zoo. This is in the Bible, Ruth May reports knowingly. She confidently divides the world into black and white, just as she has been taught.

Rachel, the vain, blond beauty, comes next. As the oldest, her voice is strong and her point of view is clear. She's a typical 1950s American teen, looking forward to celebrating her "sweet sixteen." Her speech is filled with hilarious malapropisms: she's in "the sloop of despond," ready to

> ## "Sending a girl to college is like pouring water in your shoes… it's hard to say which is worse, seeing it run out and waste the water, or seeing it hold in and wreck the shoes."

"give up the goat." Direct in her criticism and contempt for what she encounters in Africa, Rachel finds everything primitive beyond belief. The dirt, grit, and noise are all impossible. She's shocked and sarcastic about the nakedness of the natives and their strange forms of dress and undress. To her, the celebratory feast that Kilanga Village prepares to welcome her family is stupid clamor followed by disgusting food. Rachel is not all teenage disdain, however. She is also refreshingly and surprisingly critical of her father.

Last to speak is silent Adah, who sees the Congo as a parade of colors and shapes. She views the world in poetic and beautiful ways and reports what she sees in her own idiosyncratic language. Adah has fierce and private perceptions, which she keeps to herself. She and Leah are twins, but due to a mishap at birth, Adah is plagued by a limp and speaks very little. She's aware of the difficulties of her condition, but also aware of the benefits—she's left alone to think and read what she likes.

Nathan Price's voice, aggressive and determined, leaps off the page. Yet we never hear it directly, only through the testimony of the girls and Orleanna. Nathan is certain in the righteousness of his mission—to bring Jesus to the savages of Africa, to baptize them in the true god. He's also outspoken about the incompetence of women. They're dull-witted cows, and educating them is an utter waste. Nathan's similarly certain about farming methods, confidently planting his crop as if he were still in Georgia. He uses the Bible as a form of discipline, punishing his girls with "The Verse," a hundred verses copied from the Bible, the hundredth containing the lesson that suits the girls' crime.

Nathan learns lessons with varying degrees of speed. Almost immediately, he learns that the poisonwood plant he touched while cultivating his garden has given him a terrible infection. Fairly quickly, he realizes that his planting methods are incompatible with the Congo's soil and climate. But it takes Nathan a full six months to appreciate that the river where he wishes to baptize his flock is fatally dangerous—a crocodile ate a child in the river. Nathan does not always learn from experience, though. While he suffers humiliations, he is unable to draw conclusions from them. He stubbornly forges ahead on his righteous path.

The first book of *The Poisonwood Bible* sets the pattern of alternating voices, each one conveying layers of information about the speaker, her position in the family, the America of memory, the Congo of personal experience. Layers of meaning in each voice then weave together into a fabric of many voices. Layers upon layers of past experience, prejudice, knowledge, hope and desire are brought to bear on the present confrontation with the Congo. Each character, in describing the African present, also describes the American past and the family dynamic.

The world of the Congo, strange at first, becomes stranger still—but at the same time becomes more and more familiar. We journey into Leah's Congo, as well as Adah's, Rachel's, and Ruth May's. We come to understand Nathan's strict, rigid outlook and Orleanna's exhausted struggle with the day-to-day. Bit by bit, we piece together a sense of what the Congo is like, what its people believe in, what their behavior means, and what their words mean. But these revelations unfurl in a story that is ever shifting shape.

BOOK TWO: THE REVELATION THE THINGS WE LEARNED, KILANGA, JUNE 30, 1960

Book Two reveals, in bits and pieces, the political situation in the Congo. Kingsolver constructs a clear parallel between the political deterioration in the Congo and the familial deterioration in the Price household. The girls begin to make some sense of the things they see, hear, and overhear. They see armed Belgian soldiers along with motley groups of young men in tattered clothes marching and training. They hear news of the larger political world—the Belgians, the Russian Communists, the American president—all of whom have their own ideas about what's best for the Congo. The girls hear the name Patrice Lumumba and are told that an election is coming up in May and a declaration of independence coming up on June 30.

Ruth May recounts the atrocities committed in the rubber plantations and the diamond mines, where men and children have their hands cut off and are beaten and killed. They learn that the native children can't go to school (just as blacks are barred from attending college back home in the South). Ignorance, submission and servitude are the prescribed paths for the Congolese natives, just as marriage is the correct path for girls.

During a visit from the Underdowns, a family from the Baptist ministry, the Prices learn just how grave the situation is. The Prices' replacements at the ministry aren't coming. The Underdowns advise the Prices to leave and are themselves planning an escape. But Nathan Price, steadfast in his dangerous and unsound beliefs, refuses to leave. Against all evidence to the contrary, he remains confident that he's helping the natives.

As the political situation becomes increasingly dire, so does the family situation in the Price household. Orleanna, while still afraid, draws closer to open rebellion. She begins to see what her children have already grasped. Her husband is not only unconcerned about the family's well-being and safety, but truly willing to put them—and keep them—at risk. Orleanna's duty as a mother is now in direct opposition to her duty as a wife, to her husband's mission to remain in the Congo. The girls admit that their father is crazy.

Much of the girls' information comes from Anatole, an educated native introduced into the family as the interpreter of Nathan's sermons and the teacher of young children. Anatole disagrees openly with Nathan and tries to explain the religious beliefs of Tata Ndu and the rest of the community. He also comforts Leah as Orleanna and Ruth May become sicker and sicker with what is later diagnosed as malaria.

As Book Two closes, the family situation and the larger political one mirror each other even more closely than before. Nathan's women grow restless and discontented with his absolute rule, just as the African natives begin to agitate for freedom from European oppression.

BOOK THREE: THE JUDGES
THE THINGS WE DIDN'T KNOW,
KILANGA, SEPTEMBER 1960

The political and the personal both deteriorate. Katanga Province, the richest area of the Congo and the source of most of its diamonds, cobalt, copper and zinc, secedes from the Republic. Moise Tshombe leads and rules the new wealthy state. Divisions within the Price family grow deeper and graver. The bedridden Orleanna can no longer do the household chores, which fall to the ill-prepared girls. Even Leah, Nathan's most loyal follower, begins to doubt his word. A visit from Reverend Fowles, the minister who preceded Nathan, adds to the girls' doubts and fears. In contrast to Nathan's all-or-nothing approach to his mission, Reverend Fowles believes in the *relative* usefulness of Christianity in the Congo. He neither rejects the beliefs of the natives nor attempts to impose his word. Fowles has respect for Tata Ndu, who guides his village fairly and effectively.

Family rifts deepen when Tata Ndu proposes to add Rachel to his array of wives. Marriage to Tata Ndu would require Rachel to undergo ritual circumcision—"circus mission," as Ruth May innocently calls it. To reject such an offer is to cause deep cultural offense. In an attempt to extricate the family—and supposedly Rachel—from this dilemma, Nathan arranges a false engagement between Rachel and Eeben Axelroot. Though a shady character, Eeben is at least white. He participates in a number of illegal and dangerous enterprises—not simply smuggling diamonds, but working as an agent for the CIA. Axelroot boasts to Rachel that he's killed men and that he knows of a plot to assassinate Lumumba. Despite her knowledge of his unsavory character, Rachel is attracted to Eeben. She allows and even encourages his sham suit. Orleanna, meanwhile, rages ineffectually against this horrible choice.

Kingsolver juxtaposes Rachel's forced engagement against Leah's growing trust in and love for Anatole, who speaks truthfully and respectfully to her. He allows her to teach in the school and instructs her in the use of the bow and arrow, both decidedly unfeminine pursuits. Initially, Leah values Anatole for his honorable approach to religion. He translates truly, so the people have full knowledge of what they're choosing or rejecting. Unlike Nathan, Anatole doesn't need to believe—he needs to provide information. Leah's admiration turns to love when Anatole helps her family to escape from catastrophe: the attack of the ants. Her father, as usual, is useless in the situation, lecturing pompously on the flight of the Egyptians as people flee in terror.

The attack of the ants, a horrible event told from several points of view, also changes Adah. She believes her mother leaves her to die, choosing to save Ruth May instead—and indeed, it's Anatole who ultimately saves Adah. This disaster also mirrors the larger concerns of the novel: "Don't blame God for what ants have to do. We all get hungry. Congolese people are not so different from Congolese ants. . . . When they are pushed down long enough they will rise up. If they bite you, they are trying to fix things in the only way they know." Again, the small mimics the large.

At this point, the political and personal worlds of the novel are in utter chaos. Part of the newly formed Congo has seceded. Much of the rest is in revolt. The elected President Lumumba is about to be murdered. The Price women are now in open rebellion. Even Leah, the most stalwart supporter of Nathan, has succumbed to her doubts.

BOOK FOUR: BEL AND THE SERPENT WHAT WE LOST, KILANGA, JANUARY 17, 1961

Orleanna's opening recollections are almost exclusively political. She is aware now, many years later, of what was happening in the Congo when she was too busy feeding her family to notice or care. She reports the findings of the Church committee, which revealed, among many other crimes, the involvement of the CIA in the imprisonment, capture and death of Patrice Lumumba. History didn't cross Orleanna's mind then. Now it does. "Now I know, whatever your burdens, to hold yourself apart from the lot of more powerful men is an illusion."

The rest of Book Four explores several dramatic confrontations in the village. First, Tata Ndu interrupts Nathan's sermon to demand a democratic vote on whether Jesus should hold the office of personal god to Kilanga Village. Nathan, outraged at the idea, is forced to let the vote go forward. Jesus loses. Next, Leah, who now knows how to shoot with her bow and arrow, surfaces as a candidate to participate in the village hunt. Democratic vote again is used to decide this controversial question. With Anatole's support, Leah wins the right to be the first woman to hunt, by a vote of fifty-one to forty-five. But Nathan, who still rules by patriarchal authority, forbids her. Leah flatly disobeys him and joins the hunt. Then, when Leah kills a young impala during the hunt and one of Tata Ndu's sons tries to take credit, Nelson, one of Anatole's students, defends Leah and insults the son by calling him a woman. In revenge, Tata Kuvudundu plants a poisonous mamba snake in the chicken house where Nelson sleeps. The mamba, discovered through a clever trap the girls devise, kills the innocent Ruth May as it makes its escape from the chicken house.

Ruth May's death liberates and energizes Orleanna—it is the tragedy she needed to justify her rebellion. She muses on "waiting for that ax to fall so I could walk away with no forgiveness in my heart." Moving unhindered like a force of nature, Orleanna prepares the body of her youngest child for burial, then systematically gives away her possessions. When the village children gather to regard Ruth May's body, Nathan baptizes them. He worries only that Ruth May herself was never baptized. Nathan is profoundly out of touch with the children, with the village, and with his family.

BOOK FIVE: EXODUS
WHAT WE CARRIED OUT

Orleanna begins with a maternal lament. Still trying to find forgiveness, she tells the story of women's lives, women who wash floors and prepare meals as men form committees to bring down governments. "*Conquest* and *liberation* and *democracy* and *divorce* are words that mean squat, basically, when you have hungry children and clothes to get out on the line and it looks like rain." Like the Congo itself, Orleanna bears her losses as gracefully as she can. And loss and sorrow are all she has.

In a wrathful and frenetic state following Ruth May's death, Orleanna gathers her girls and literally walks away from their life in the Congo. This formidable woman cannot be denied, and the girls have no choice but to follow her. They walk toward Leopoldville, helped along the way by village women, friends and relatives of women from Kilanga. The girls are drenched by rain and besieged with cold and hunger. But they make it to Bulungu, where they meet Eeben Axelroot and his plane.

After their escape together, the Price women go their separate ways. Rachel takes off with Axelroot. Anatole cares for Leah, who has developed malaria on the long trek. Orleanna and Adah find transport back to

> *"Illusions mistaken for truth are the pavement under our feet. They are what we call civilization."*

the States. Leah decides to stay with Anatole, who promises to love and protect her although she is still too young to marry. While Anatole fights against Mobutu's forces and later is imprisoned by them, Leah hides in a convent of French nuns. Released after three years of imprisonment without formal charges, Anatole marries Leah. Together they have four sons. Anatole, despite many dangers, continues his belief in genuine independence and maintains his loyalty to the secret Parti Lumumbist Unifié. Leah becomes an English teacher. Upon returning from a visit to the United States to see Orleanna, Anatole is arrested again. Freed at last, he receives offers for positions in the government but declines.

Rachel throws in her lot with Axelroot, who lives with her as her husband but evades actual marriage. They live in white South Africa, where Rachel easily fits into the white society: she contentedly purchases Breck shampoo and Campbell's tomato soup. As Axelroot treats her like his slave-girlfriend-housemaid, Rachel finds someone better—the first attaché to the French embassy—and moves to Brazzaville, French Congo, with him. When the attaché leaves Rachel for his mistress, she finds a third husband, Remy Fairly, who has the "decency to die" quickly and leave her the Equatorial, a posh hotel. Running the hotel on her own suits Rachel very well. She remains unchanged—still proud of her blond beauty, uncomprehending of her mother's sorrow, and her sisters' noble efforts to make amends and produce change.

Adah, back in Georgia, convinces Emory University to accept her, first as an undergraduate and then as a medical student. While in the States, she cures herself of her limp and her other impediments. And she forgives her mother. She becomes an expert in tropical epidemiology and returns to Africa.

Orleanna grows flowers. Nathan, we learn, is solitary, wild-haired, struggling against malnutrition and parasites. Eventually he disappears into the forest. Later, we hear a report that he went to work around Lusambo and passed away there. Still later, reports say he hid from strangers, and that with his long white beard he was known as a white witch doctor named Tata Prize. One report claims he had five wives. The Price girls believe this report to be simple legend until they recognize that it was they themselves who were Nathan's five wives. A final rumor tells of Nathan baptizing children and terrorizing natives until they chased him and burned him to death.

BOOK SIX
SONG OF THE THREE CHILDREN

Rachel, now fifty, proudly cares for her complexion. She has never had children. She has taken care of herself in the ways she knows how, and she has survived. She has no regrets. Leah, after thirty years of marriage and four sons, remains productive and resourceful in the Congo, she teaches nutrition, sanitation, and the benefits of soybeans. Adah, back in Atlanta, has neither children nor pets, but viruses that she nurtures and tends. She has made important discoveries about AIDS and Ebola.

BOOK SEVEN
THE EYES IN THE TREES

Told from the heavenly perspective of Ruth May and in the voice of Africa, this brief epilogue brings forgiveness to Orleanna, granting her permission to move on. By extension, it grants all of Africa the same permission to move on into the bright future.

Voices in the Wilderness

The Price women all share the experience of life in Africa — but respond to the chaos of their situation in vastly different ways.

○　○　○

ORLEANNA

Much of Orleanna's progress is unseen and unheard. She reports only from the distance of time and space, long after the events in the Congo, from the vantage point of Sanderling Island, Georgia. But we know that she has traveled far and suffered immeasurably to get to this new vantage point. She craves forgiveness, but feels only desperate guilt.

Orleanna grew up during the Great Depression in Jackson, Missis-sippi. Her mother died when she was young, and her father, an eye doc-tor, managed to get by during those hard years. At seventeen, Orleanna met the confident and ambitious Nathan Price preaching at a Baptist tent revival. She married him and then almost immediately lost him to the Far East battleground of World War II. He returned, the only survivor of the Bataan Death March, a different man — hard, cold, determined to save more souls than were lost on the road from Bataan. In less than two years, Orleanna had three babies. Overworked, overwhelmed and oppressed, she toiled on, believing in Nathan and the lord.

Traveling to the Congo is not a choice. Orleanna follows her husband. And once in the Congo, she needs all her energy just to survive, to find food, cook meals, and provide shelter and safety for her children. Her understanding of the larger world and her husband's place in it grows over time, but it's hard to see this progress. We know that she tries to convince Nathan to leave when the Underdowns suggest it. We know that she objects to the marriage proposals for Rachel. We know that she's powerless to influence her husband. And for much of the stay in Congo, Orleanna is literally too weak to think or act, lying in bed with malaria. During the attack of the ants, she carries Ruth May away, leaving Adah behind—an act that wounds Adah deeply. Much later, Orleanna explains that a mother's duty is to save the youngest first: "When push comes to shove, a mother takes care of her children from the bottom up." Ruth May's death is the event that galvanizes Orleanna, giving her the resolve to act. And once she starts acting, she acts deliberately, relentlessly, and invincibly. She moves forward like a force of nature. She leaves Nathan without a backward glance or thought. Nothing can stop her as she marches her remaining children out of the jungle, reversing the Bataan Death March by bringing her family safely to civilization. With Adah, Orleanna returns to Georgia, where she first plants flowers, later works for civil rights, and much later, forgives herself.

Orleanna is, in many ways, the most moving character in the novel. She is the most powerless and oppressed throughout most of the story, and the most determined and focused by the end. From blindness she attains clear and painful sight. Her most important insight is her sense of her own culpability. She realizes she has stayed too long, remained too silent. She doesn't know how to name her sin—complicity? loyalty? stupefaction? But she acknowledges that she has sinned—she wasn't a senseless tool. She had a will, and she didn't use it until it was too late. At the same time, Orleanna recognizes that women like her, overwhelmed with the daily tasks of survival, can know little and do less: "I knew Rome was burning, but I had just enough water to scrub the floor, so I did what I could." Her opening chapters are moving and heartbreaking in their combination of tenderness and toughness. Her sorrow never ends.

RACHEL PRICE

The least sympathetic of the girls, Rachel is the beauty queen of the Price family. She thinks of herself in exactly this way—as an object of beauty chiefly remarkable for her coloring, fair skin, and white-blond hair. The world values her as she values herself. From the start, she's furious at being uprooted from her high school heaven and placed in a jungle hell.

She's open in her annoyance at her father and clear in expressing her contempt for him. Rachel refers to him sarcastically as "the Father Knows Best of all times." She doesn't try to please him—she tries only to please herself. Though Rachel is older than the twins, they feel superior to her intellectually. Rachel makes numerous errors in her choice of words and her knowledge of the world in general.

Rachel is outraged when Tata Ndu proposes to marry her, and doubly outraged when her father instructs her to pretend to be engaged to Eeben Axelroot. But at the same time, she's flattered and pleased by this male attention. Marriage proposals are what Rachel was raised to inspire. Beauty is her only asset, marriage her only market for selling this asset. The values of her 1950s Southern upbringing promote the idea of girls selling themselves to the highest bidder. The values of the Congo are not too different.

> The **experience** in the Congo **teaches** Rachel **nothing.**

But Rachel's preference for Axelroot over Tata Ndu is based primarily on race. She cannot imagine marrying a black man. But it seems she can imagine marrying a murderer, which Axelroot boasts he is. The circumcision issue doesn't seem to enter into her disdain for Tata Ndu's proposal—it's his color and his other wives that make him impossible. Not once does Rachel consider his character. Axelroot, on the other hand, is not only a traitor and murderer, but also a liar and betrayer, who promises but never delivers marriage. Rachel lives with him out of wedlock. She leaves him when she finds a better chance, a French diplomat, but leaves him as well when a still better opportunity presents itself—a man who conveniently dies and leaves her a luxury hotel to manage. Alone with her hotel, she tends to business and to her beauty.

The experience in the Congo teaches Rachel nothing. She understood the idea of self-preservation pretty well before the Congo, and she understands it even better afterward. She never refers to the time she spent in the Congo, never looks back, never grieves or laments. She's completely uncomprehending about the choices her sisters make. Of Leah's choice of Anatole for a husband Rachel says, "But to *marry* one [an African]? And have children? It doesn't seem natural. I can't see how those boys are any kin to me." Of Adah's profession, "she works night and day wearing a horrid white coat in some dreary big-deal place in Atlanta where they study disease organisms. Well, fine! I guess somebody has to do it!" Her mother she understands is "still moping around" about Ruth May's death. Despite Rachel's protestations, she's wounded that no member of her family seems interested in visiting her. She takes no responsibility for what happened to her family in the Congo. Her view of the horrors the family experienced there is very simple: "What happened to us in the Congo was simply the bad luck of two opposite worlds crashing into each other, causing tragedy."

ADAH PRICE

Though a twin, Adah is an outlier, the most unusual and different member of the Price family, the most remote. She is the "damaged" twin whose brain failed to develop properly, leaving her with a limp and without a voice. Initially defined by her medical condition, she overcomes it to become a medical practitioner herself. Adah is mute during the central action of the story, but we hear her voice through her words on the page. In fact, words are her strong suit: she plays with language, reading words and whole books backward and forward, inventing words, creating palindromes. She's often more interested in language than in action, concentrating on the meanings of words, especially the multiple and often contradictory meanings of words. Through language, she gains access to the culture.

Adah thinks of herself as a monster, a crooked creature. But she also thinks of herself as gifted, special, possessing a rare and singular intelligence. It's Adah who notices that *bangala* means both "precious" and "poisonwood." When Nathan says that Jesus is *bangala*, he pronounces it unintentionally as "poisonwood," not as "precious." This is the gospel he preaches, the poisonwood gospel.

Adah's most dramatic moments are nonevents. In the first, a lion does not eat her as she walks on a jungle path. The village presumes her dead when they find the lion's tracks and hers together. But Adah is miraculously saved, as the lion eats a young bushbuck instead. Later, during the attack of the ants, Adah has another important nonevent, as her mother does not save her, choosing to save Ruth May instead. Though Anatole ultimately saves Adah, she has witnessed her mother choose the perfect

Ruth May and leave Adah to be further damaged: "That night marks my life's dark center, the moment when growing up ended and the long downward slope toward death began." Much later, Adah learns from her mother the law of motherhood, that a mother saves her children from the bottom up. When Adah learns that her mother's action wasn't based on preference or choice, but rather maternal law, she accepts this and forgives her mother. Later, when Orleanna leads her daughters out of the Congo, it is Adah she takes with her, Adah she holds onto.

Back in the United States, Adah talks her way into Emory University, first as an undergraduate, then as a medical student. Yes, she talks. She overcomes her mute status and eventually gives up her crippled status as well. She makes herself whole. She becomes the scientist she always believed she could become, briefly visits Africa, then settles in Atlanta to study infectious diseases. She doesn't have children or pets—instead, she has the viruses that she studies lovingly. It's Adah who says that the family produced a clear-eyed scientist (herself), a penitent (Leah), a shrewd minor politician (Rachel), and a ghost (Ruth May).

Adah has her own fierce energy. She has clear sight and keen perceptions. She tells the truth. From a bitter, betrayed and angry child, she grows into a strong, focused and caring woman. She loses her slant—but gains direction.

LEAH PRICE

The most complex and committed of the Price girls, Leah is the one we identify with the most. Like her father she is an idealist. Like her father she is burdened by guilt—he for surviving Bataan, she for surviving intact while her twin, Adah, suffered damage at birth. At first, Leah is her father's most loyal supporter. She wants more than anything to win his favor and remain firmly in it. She admires his faith and endeavors to imitate it. Slowly and through experience, Leah's faith in her father's judgment wanes until she becomes his most vocal and ardent critic. Eventually, she becomes the enemy of all he believed in. A character of extremes, Leah becomes an idealist of another kind. As she maintains her commitment to ideals and beliefs, she remains, in a sense, her father's truest daughter. She wants to believe in her father and only slowly and reluctantly comes to recognize that he is mistaken.

17

Leah shares in her father's early defeats in planting the African soil. She's by his side in Leopoldville to watch the inauguration of Patrice Lumumba. But she alone is awed and moved. When Nathan refuses to pack up and go when everyone else says that missionaries should leave Africa, Leah begins to doubt his judgment seriously. He has made many misjudgments and hasn't protected her mother or sister from illness. Leah has seen him bluster, blunder and fail. When doubt enters her mind, the Congo becomes a fearsome place for her: "All my life I've tried to set my shoes squarely into his footprints. . . ."

A tomboy from the start, Leah eagerly learns to shoot with a bow and arrow when Anatole offers her the chance. She's happy to learn to shoot and thrilled to be asked to join the hunt. When her father forbids her to join the men, she openly disobeys him. She participates in the hunt despite opposition from many of the men of the village, kills a young male impala, and insists on claiming the kill. Nelson forcefully defends her. Every one of these willful acts leads to trouble, including an attempt on Nelson's life that results in the death of the innocent Ruth May. The hunt, meant to be a time of triumph, turns to bitter quarrelling and discord.

What Leah doesn't learn through direct experience she learns through Anatole, who teaches her patiently and lovingly. She's eager to learn, open to his lessons. After doubting her father, she needs something to believe in. When Orleanna leads the remaining girls out of the Congo, Leah goes as far as Bulungu, where Anatole meets her and nurses her back to health. She has been falling in love with him for some time, but now admits it for the first time. She

Where Leah had been her father's supporter and defender, she becomes Anatole's.

believes him to be goodness itself, and he believes her to be truest truth. Anatole reassembles the shattered Leah, delivering her through her life. They eventually marry and have four sons. Anatole becomes Leah's cause. While he fights for African independence, she hides in safety in a convent. When he's imprisoned for his opposition to Mobutu, she waits patiently for him, raising her sons, teaching women. Where Leah had been her father's supporter and defender, she becomes Anatole's.

Leah's slow conversion from her father's unthinking tool to Anatole's free and faithful wife is beautifully and carefully accomplished. Leah becomes her own thinking and feeling person. She reassembles herself out of her shattered family, using her experience to understand who she was and who she is capable of being.

RUTH MAY PRICE

Though only five years old during the main action of the novel, Ruth May is the first to establish communication with her peers in Kilanga. Brave and clever, she organizes games with the local children, including her favorite, "Mother, May I." She becomes the chief of the children in Kilanga. Ruth May's naïve point of view is perfect for reporting without judgment what she hears from the adults around her and what she sees with her own eyes. She cheerfully reports on the Jim Crow laws back home in Georgia, which separate whites from blacks. She's proud to know the Bible story that tells that the descendants of Ham are destined to be slaves forever. When Ruth May breaks her arm falling out of a tree and is transported by Eeben Axelroot's plane to see the doctor in Stanleyville, she sees and hears more than she ought to, more than she's supposed to understand. She sees the African army marching, she hears the name Lumumba, she sees Axelroot's diamonds and whiskey. She may not know how to interpret what she sees and hears, but she reports with innocent clarity.

Refusing to take her malaria pills, Ruth May falls ill and spends a great deal of time in bed with her mother. Ill and weak, she dies not from malaria but from the bite of the mamba snake that's planted with the intent to kill Nelson. It's Ruth May's death that moves Orleanna to act, to leave Nathan and the Congo. It's her death that haunts Orleanna and her ghost that speaks in the final book of *The Poisonwood Bible*.

NATHAN PRICE

Nathan has no narrating voice in the novel, but he has a dominant voice in the story nonetheless. He is all arrogant certainty. He believes in Jesus and in his mission to bring Jesus to the savages of Africa. He has no consideration for the beliefs and practices of the natives. He insists on taking his wife and daughters to a remote African village where they are ill prepared to cope with the conditions. He does nothing to help them adjust or survive because he's too busy helping the natives—people who neither want nor need his help. Nathan is capable of learning a little, as we see when he makes small changes to his planting scheme when he loses his crop, but he's not capable of learning much. Though he gives up his idea of baptism in the river when he finally learns that the native women have reason to fear crocodiles, he gives up little else of his agenda. He seems not to notice as his family falls apart around him. When his wife and youngest daughter take to their beds, he pays no heed. He dismisses all warnings (from the Underdowns, from Reverend Fowles) to leave the Congo, stubbornly remaining steadfast to his divine mission. We don't know Nathan's reaction to the death of Ruth May and the desertion of his family. We never actually see him again, but only hear wild rumors of his eccentric behavior, madness and eventual death. He becomes a creature of myth—the mad white doctor.

The only explanation for his character is his wartime history, the burden of being the sole survivor of the death march to Bataan. He feels the need to save more souls than were lost in Bataan and the need to stay at his post. But even this explanation is hardly adequate to explain Nathan's stubborn refusal to understand that his message is unwanted and unheeded, his methods useless and offensive. He remains a shrill, simplistic, lone voice, initially certain and severe, later wild and lost. Nathan is the American fundamentalist family equivalent of the European colonial presence in Africa. He carries a huge burden of allegorical weight. And at times, he feels more like an allegorical embodiment of evil than a man.

Out of Africa

Kingsolver's novel masterfully intertwines questions of religion and politics, marriage and motherhood, language and madness.

○ ○ ○

How do the two major strands of the novel—the Price family's disintegration and the Congo's struggle for independence—fit together?

"KINGSOLVER CRAFTS TWO STORIES OF THE STRONG DOMINATING THE WEAK."

The two story lines in *The Poisonwood Bible* are two manifestations of the same evil—the strong dominating the weak until the weak rebel. Nathan, the all-powerful man in the Price family, directs the destinies of his wife and all his daughters. He's the unquestioned leader and teacher, and the women in his family have no choice but to follow him. They must obey, even when it's clear that Nathan is not only indifferent to their best interests but actually willing to subject them to discomfort, illness, and even death. The Price women break away from Nathan only after a tragedy, the death of Ruth May, emboldens Orleanna to rebel.

For this part of Africa, it's much the same. The Congo lives under white, European colonial rule and is subject to exploitation and virtual slavery. The Congolese are unable to break away until conditions become intolerable and a leader, Patrice Lumumba, comes forward to guide them. Yet even with a leader and a brief taste of independence, they fall back into misery, poverty, and slavery. But the two stories—the personal and the political—mirror one another in many ways. Both stories reveal the same inequity.

"THE PRICE FAMILY STORY IS A POLITICAL ALLEGORY."

Kingsolver intends the events in the Price family to shed light on the larger political events in Africa and the world. The Prices carry with them to Africa a whole set of beliefs about technology, politics, religion, agriculture, and health, just as European nations carried a series of beliefs into the countries they colonized. The colonizers then set about arrogantly imposing these beliefs on cultures that didn't want or need them.

Just like the European imperialists, the Prices are repeatedly rebuffed and defeated in their attempts to sell themselves and their ideas. Nathan, the chief exporter of beliefs (religious and agricultural), fails miserably over and over again to make either his plants or his congregation grow. Nonetheless, he perseveres, unaware that he's being undermined and even mocked. Eventually Nathan is completely defeated and overthrown. The Price women are more sensitive to their mistakes and are willing to admit failure, and they adapt gradually in the face of their surroundings. They're flexible, open to change, and therefore fare better in their new environment. The allegory is obvious: to succeed in a strange land one must be sensitive to difference and flexible in response to it. Values and beliefs that are forced, onto people or soil, will never take root.

"THE PRICES' STORY AND THE POLITICAL STORY ARE MIRROR IMAGES."

The two stories mirror each other. They're not exact reflections of each other, but they do shed light on one another. The family reflects the political, just as the political reflects the familial. Kingsolver weaves the two stories together in beautiful and enlightening ways.

The Price girls live with stifling rules and laws. They aren't allowed to study or go to college. They're raised to marry, not to do anything else—or even consider doing anything else. Parents and culture alike discourage independent thought in the girls; following men is the prescribed path. Africans are diminished in the same way: they are denied education and forced to follow European laws and rules of conduct. The Price girls are frustrated and angry, just as the Congolese are. Like the Congolese, the girls have no means of redress. Escape and rebellion are their only options.

We see the girls slowly learn the limitations of their position, struggle against it, and eventually find their individual ways to surmount or succumb to it. The Africans, we assume, go through this same process, although we don't see it as clearly or closely. We make the leap from the girls and their oppression in the family to the Congolese and their oppression by the Belgians. In some places the leap is easy to make, in others it's more difficult. The beauty of *The Poisonwood Bible* is the subtlety of these moves. Some are small and simple, some vast and complicated. To see connections and similarities where they didn't appear at first is one of Kingsolver's great gifts to us.

O   O   O

What role does Christianity play in the novel?

"NATHAN'S BRAND OF CHRISTIANITY IS WHOLLY DESTRUCTIVE."

Nathan's idea of Christianity—a mission to impose itself on a people who don't want it or need it—is utterly destructive. Nathan seeks to brand the Congolese natives with his god and denies their customs and beliefs entirely. At first, he seems simply silly in this attempt. Later, he seems obstinate, and later still, he comes across as insane. As Kingsolver herself has said, Nathan is "an arrogant proselytizer." Nathan dominates as surely as do the colonial powers, but he does so with the tool of Christianity. Here in Africa, as elsewhere, this kind of imposition is destructive, a means of control and an expression of contempt. Nathan uses the Bible as a punishment—he hands out the "Verse" to the girls to correct their slips in obedience, understanding, or faith. Nathan's Christianity swells into a mania, a belief system devoid of flexibility or room for growth. Even as Nathan fails to harvest food or souls, he charges ahead. Christianity is an obsession for him—one that proves dangerous.

"CHRISTIANITY CAN BE A FORCE FOR GOOD."

Reverend Fowles, the former missionary in Kilanga, is a good, Christian man who is open-minded to forms of spirituality other than Christianity. He rejoices in nature. He believes that the Congolese are truly his brothers —in fact, he has married an African woman. He sees himself as a branch that's been grafted on to African roots. When Orleanna tells him that the Mission League cut off the stipend for her husband's mission right before independence, Brother Fowles replies, "For certain, Mrs. Price, there are Christians and then there are Christians." A true Christian, Fowles receives and happily accepts support from a wide group of benefactors, including the National Geographic Society. He accepts the native beliefs of the Congo as well as the truth of Christianity. He's a truly spiritual man, and his appearance in the novel speaks for Christianity as a healing force in the world. His part in the story is small but significant. Christianity doesn't have to take the form of Nathan's arrogant and blind proselytizing. It doesn't need to be narrow, exclusive, or punishing—it can be caring, embracing, and accepting. Whereas Nathan dismisses Tata Ndu as a heathen, Brother Fowles treats him with respect, saying of him, "As a Christian, I respect his judgments. He guides his village fairly, all things considered."

"LIKE MANY BELIEFS, RELIGIOUS IDEAS CAN BE USED FOR GOOD OR EVIL."

Religious beliefs can be used toward beneficial or harmful ends. Nathan's form of Christianity is certainly evil in the novel. It does no one good, not even Nathan himself. It hurts him, his family, and his congregation. On the other hand, the beliefs of the people of Kilanga, led by Tata Ndu, help the village to survive a grueling life and to understand the world. Kingsolver suggests that beliefs formed on native soil are the best, the strongest, the truest. Beliefs imported from afar and imposed by force are suspect.

But evil can exist even in indigenous religions. The subjugation of women is a part of both Christianity and the Congolese religion. Female circumcision and multiple wives are honored customs in parts of Africa. According to Nathan, the separation of the races in the American South and the denial of equal rights to blacks are justified by the Bible. Any religion can be used to justify exclusionary and unjust ideas. Any system can become evil when rigidly applied. Brother Fowles, who accepts the good and rejects the bad, always faces the world with a varied and flexible response that's the hallmark of a truly spiritual man. Anatole is also a man of true spirituality: he believes in giving people many ideas so that they can decide for themselves what's best for them.

○ ○ ○

What does the novel say about marriage?

"TRADITIONAL MARRIAGES LIKE THE PRICES' ARE TERRIBLE."

Nathan and Orleanna's marriage adheres to the mores of the time. In the 1950s, Southern girls stitched pillowcases for their hope chests and waited for the right man to come along and carry them away. At first, Nathan seems to be the right man for Orleanna. He has energy and enthusiasm for his work. He courts Orleanna with fervor. But even then, when they marry they hardly know themselves or one another. Orleanna does what a proper Southern bride is supposed to do—obey her husband, follow him, support him. She does so until she recognizes that she's followed a man who will lead her and her children into death and destruction. She learns to question too late. She's unprepared to think for herself. Orleanna waits and waits for a final blow that will allow her to leave without guilt, and when that final blow comes, she doesn't look back.

"UNTRADITIONAL MARRIAGES CAN HOLD JOY AND BEAUTY."

Leah slowly learns to love Anatole for who he is, for who she believes him to be. She admires his ideals, courage, and honesty. She loves him despite the fact that he's deeply marked on the face and that he's a black African, which her upbringing has told her is an inappropriate match for her. Leah loves Anatole for who he is inside. She says of their marriage, "marriage is one long fit of compromise, deep and wide. There is always one agenda swallowing another, a squeaky wheel crying out. But hasn't our life together meant more to the world than either of us could have meant alone?" She understands marriage as a give-and-take experience, a sharing of insight, intelligence, and opinion. This vision is utterly unlike the marriage of her parents, in which one parent does all the thinking. Leah shares in Anatole's vision and supports him in it, not because she thinks that's what a wife is supposed to do, but because she herself believes in that vision. Leah's idea that marriage should mean more than a life alone, that marriage adds significance and beauty to life, is beautiful in itself. She's still an idealist like her father. She wants to believe in something larger than herself. And marriage provides her with that scope — not just a husband and children, but a just cause to believe in and fight for.

"MARRIAGE CAN FUNCTION AS A BUSINESS TOOL OR STRATEGY."

Rachel uses men and marriage to get what she wants and needs. She uses Eeben Axelroot to get her away from her family and out of Katanga. She uses the French diplomat to give her legitimacy and social status. Her final husband gives her money and, after his death, a business to manage. Men provide Rachel with life and livelihood. Beauty is her currency, and she spends it to buy security. She never expresses any interest in the men themselves, any attraction to their bodies, any respect for their minds. She cares only about what they can do for her materially and socially. Children, needless to say, are not part of Rachel's plan. Her marriages are business arrangements, nothing more. But within this framework, Rachel is shrewd, a survivor, and she chooses her husbands well. They do provide her with what she needs. Her acute business sense pays off, and she supports herself well from the inherited hotel. Marriage serves her exactly as she expected and hoped it would. It makes her life secure — empty, perhaps, but safe.

Why does Orleanna act as she does, complying with her husband and then rebelling?

"SHE'S A PROPER 1950s SOUTHERN GIRL TAUGHT TO OBEY HER MAN."

Orleanna married young and followed her husband. He made the decisions, she obeyed. She takes her family to the Congo without a thought because that's what her husband decides to do. The idea of disobeying Nathan never occurs to her until hardship and tragedy galvanize her. She waits for, even longs for, the right moment, the dramatic event that enables her to rebel: "Strange to say, when it came I felt as if I'd been waiting for it my whole married life. Waiting for that ax to fall so I could walk away with no forgiveness in my heart." Unfortunately, the pivotal event is the death of Ruth May. It takes the death of Orleanna's youngest to spur her into action. For many good, proper Christian women, even this provocation might not have been enough to warrant disobedience or flight. Orleanna married at a time when women had simple hopes. She doesn't expect companionship or joy, just survival for herself and her children.

"SHE'S TOO EXHAUSTED BY THE URGENT DAY-TO-DAY TASKS TO ASK THE LARGER QUESTIONS."

The simple day-to-day chores of life in the Congo—finding food, preparing meals, keeping the house clean and safe—are so taxing that Orleanna doesn't have the time or strength to think about anything else. She's focused on the urgent daily tasks and can't consider how her children may be suffering in other, less visible ways. Keeping them fed and healthy is all she can manage. Orleanna is deathly ill and too weak to get out of bed for long stretches of time. She asks herself why she stayed so long. Was her sin a failure of virtue or of competence? She admits that she was too focused on the daily chores to notice the larger events. "I knew Rome was burning, but I had just enough water to scrub the floor, so I did what I could."

○ ○ ○

Is the world of the novel believable?

"YES, ESPECIALLY BECAUSE OF THE MULTIPLE POINTS OF VIEW."

One of the greatest strengths of *The Poisonwood Bible* is the degree to which it seems real and true. The multiple points of view create layers of meaning that intersect with one another and form a dense reality. The points of view are never directly contradictory and never cause us to doubt that an event happened. But the girls' different judgments cause us to hold events and opinions in suspension, waiting for more information and possibly resolution.

As in our lives, when we read *The Poisonwood Bible*, we have to suspend judgment, revise opinion, develop a firm perspective over time and from many sources. Ruth May often reports events she doesn't understand, forcing us to draw our own conclusions. We read around and through Rachel's foolish and selfish assessments of people. At the same time, Rachel's a keen (if oversensitive) observer of her surroundings. Her senses are honed to taste, smell, and sound. Her feminine modesty is quick to notice nudity and immodest behavior. All of these viewpoints contribute to the vividness of Kingsolver's fictional world.

Kingsolver calls upon us to balance the various points of view, to create a coherent whole out of multiple takes on reality. When we leave *The Poisonwood Bible*, we leave a full, rich world. This is one of the novel's great accomplishments. The girls' different interests also compose a broad, textured landscape: one girl notices words, one the physical world, one the moral universe, and so on. These different perspectives lend depth and believability.

"NO, THE ALLEGORY RENDERS SOME OF THE CHARACTERS FLAT."

Although the events in the novel are realistic, a few of the characters sometimes feel flat. Nathan especially seems to be an unreal character.

Real evil people are never this utterly dark. But for the allegorical plot to work, Nathan needs to be thoroughly evil. As a character, though, he feels unreal, especially in contrast to the Price girls, who are so alive.

At the other end of the spectrum, Anatole feels a little unreal in his goodness, self-sacrifice, compassion, and understanding. Again, for the sake of allegory, he needs to be all of these things. But he doesn't feel like a real man. Perhaps if these men had greater voices, narrating voices, they would be more realistic. But as the novel stands, Nathan and Anatole feel contrived to fit the plot demands.

"YES, THE GIRLS' INNOCENCE MAKES THEIR OBSERVATIONS ESPECIALLY REAL AND TRUSTWORTHY."

Because the girls often don't know what they are telling us, we trust them to be telling the truth. They're too naïve to have ulterior motives or to be hiding information. They're too young and innocent to be double-dealing with us. And they convey much more information than they realize. When they describe the Congo, they reveal a great deal about Georgia and America. Coming from a segregated part of America, they assume the superiority of white people and the foolishness of the African natives. As white Americans, they feel they know more about everything. They don't ever need to say this explicitly—it permeates their narratives. When the girls describe life in the Congo, their point of reference and comparison is a childish view of America. They're supremely believable, creating not only a believable present in Africa but also a believable past in Georgia.

○ ○ ○

Are the characters believable?

"YES, ESPECIALLY THE ADOLESCENT GIRLS."

The voices of the girls are not only believable as real adolescent girls, they're also delightful and spirited. Rachel with her malapropisms and her general lack of knowledge of the world is very funny. Leah's devotion to her father, her desire to remain his favorite, is touching and true to life. Adah's word play is imaginative and clever and utterly personal. Ruth May's childish and innocent delight in the other children and her own ability to lead them is lovely. And the voices are utterly distinct in tone, diction, and rhythm. They are complete individuals.

"NO, NATHAN ISN'T REMOTELY BELIEVABLE."

Nathan is the one character who feels one-dimensional. He's completely blind to his family and to his congregation throughout the novel, and he never grows. Kingsolver restricts his character to blindness, arrogance, and ignorance. Nathan is in the novel to play a part—the part of evil, the counterpart to the evil Europeans who have plundered and exploited Africa. He doesn't feel like a real man but more like an allegorical figure, an embodiment of evil. Nathan's one-dimensional quality is a real weakness in the novel, because he's such an important character and because the rest of the characters feel so real, so fully conceived in comparison.

"RACHEL ALSO FALLS FLAT AS A CHARACTER."

Rachel's just as one-dimensional as her father. She's silly and vain and never seems to learn anything. The experience in the Congo appears to have no effect on her whatsoever. She's simply a silly, pretty, selfish girl who grows into a silly, pretty, selfish woman. Whereas the other girls mature and change, Rachel remains static. Like Nathan, she is in the novel to serve a purpose. Hers is to be the voice of the stereotypical white, self-satisfied woman of the American South. Although Rachel's voice is real in many ways, her position in the novel feels artificial.

○ ○ ○

What's the relationship between Kingsolver's life and the novel?

"THERE'S NO PERSONAL RELATIONSHIP—IT'S A RESEARCHED HISTORICAL NOVEL."

Kingsolver lived in central Africa for part of a year during her childhood. She has said that the experience of living in Africa, without running water, television, or any other modern comforts, was extremely powerful for her. As part of a tiny white minority in her community, she learned how it felt to be a true outsider.

But aside from these few personal experiences, *The Poisonwood Bible* is the product of historical research and imaginative invention. Kingsolver has said that she spent a great deal of time and energy researching the novel, reading many books, immersing herself in African culture through materials in libraries and museums. She read the King James Bible to capture the cadence of the Price family's speech patterns and studied the Congolese languages in a huge two-volume Kikongo-French dictionary, hoping to understand that subtle and easily misunderstood language.

In the author's note at the beginning of the novel, Kingsolver writes, "[The] characters are pure inventions with no relations on this earth, as far as I know. But the Congo in which I placed them is genuine." She goes on to thank her parents for being "different in every way from the parents I created for the narrators of this tale." In light of these words, it seems clear that Kingsolver has drawn general ideas about her African setting from her childhood experience, but that her stay in no way resembled the experiences of the characters in the novel. In this regard, the novel is complete fiction.

"THERE'S NO RELATION TO KINGSOLVER'S LIFE— IT'S PURELY ALLEGORICAL FICTION."

The Poisonwood Bible is allegory. Its relation to life is even more remote than simple invention. The novel is an invention that creates coincidence and coherence within a larger structure. Kingsolver's overall scheme for the novel includes a political allegory in which the situation in the Price family reflects the situation in the larger political world of the

Congo. Just as the Prices bring with them a set of beliefs that they intend to graciously give to (or forcibly impose on) the villagers of Kilanga, so did the Europeans impose their belief systems on Africa. The need to make this allegory work shaped much of the event and character of the novel. There's no room for personal reference where these kinds of allegorical demands must be met.

"KINGSOLVER CARES ABOUT THE PLIGHT OF WOMEN."

Many of Kingsolver's novels feature women who feel powerless, disenfranchised, uneducated, unprepared to function alone in the world. The five Price women are five such women—they embody a struggle about which Kingsolver feels deeply and personally. Parts of herself and her inner experience are in all the girls, even if her outward experience is at odds with the characters' lives. We can perceive Kingsolver in the deeply committed Leah and in the outcast Adah. And we can hear her voice as she feels guilt and remorse and takes responsibility through Orleanna at the end of the novel. When Orleanna says that she should have done more—seen more fully, acted with more alacrity—we hear Kingsolver herself.

"THERE IS A PERSONAL RELATIONSHIP TO AFRICA AND THE DIFFICULTIES OF FAMILY LIFE THERE."

We know that Kingsolver spent time in Africa as a child. She was sensitive to her surroundings and aware of the inequities of the society around her. The relationship between the events of the novel and the events of Kingsolver's life is tenuous, but a piece of her experience is in many of the characters, in their reactions and responses. Clearly, she identifies with Leah and with the need to feel a part of something larger and more meaningful than the everyday. She also identifies with Orleanna, a woman and mother, whose job it is to keep her children alive. Keeping children safe overwhelms all of Orleanna's other concerns. Women tend to children in oppressive regimes, under cruel rulers, and have little time or thought to give to the political situation in which they live. This quandary—how to balance the immediate needs of family with the larger historical events—is real and powerful to Kingsolver. One of the most powerful statements of the novel is that no one, especially women, can feel above politics, can afford to be detached from the political world.

○ ○ ○

What does the novel say about language?

"LANGUAGE IS UNSTABLE."

Kingsolver shows us again and again that language isn't always the most precise and reliable tool for conveying meaning. The language of the Congo is replete with multiple and contradictory meanings, which makes it very difficult for the Prices to understand what's going on around them. Anatole is crucial in translating the Kikongo language for the Prices and translating English for the Congolese.

Nathan Price is the only one in the novel who thinks he has a lock on the absolute meaning of everything—he believes he's the carrier of Truth and the Word of God. This arrogance is his greatest failing, and it's an indication of his supreme arrogance that he continues to believe this to the end. Nathan repeatedly makes a fool of himself by using the word *bangala* (which has especially interesting contradictory meanings) to mean "precious" but mispronounces it in a way that gives it the meaning "poisonwood." It's Anatole, who's especially sensitive to language, who translates Nathan's sermons as faithfully as he can so that the people can understand what Nathan's saying and decide for themselves if they think he's speaking the Truth. Brother Fowles, on his visit to Prices, is humble about his ability to know the Truth. He expresses doubts about the translation of the Bible, asking Leah, "Did you think God wrote it all down in the English of King James himself?" Leah has never been encouraged to think about the word of God in this way, and she suddenly begins to consider that her father may be very mistaken.

In the author's note at the beginning of the novel, Kingsolver writes, "I couldn't have written the book at all without two remarkable sources of literary inspiration, approximately equal in size: K.E. Laman's *Dictionnaire Kikongo-Français*, and the King James Bible." And in other places she remarks that she studied the King James version of the Bible to make sure she had the cadence of the Price family speech correctly. She studied the Kikongo language extensively to understand the complex pattern of meanings of that language. She recognizes in many places and in many ways that language is crucial to the novel, to how the characters express themselves, communicate with one another, and misunderstand one another.

"LANGUAGE CAN BE USED AS A FORM OF PLAY."

Adah is an inventor and juggler of language. She uses it to comfort and amuse herself in her mute and isolated state. Language is a solace to her. Puns, word games, palindromes, the multiple and odd meanings of words all delight her. Language is Adah's private source of humor and amusement. To Adah, language is play, words linked through sound patterns and rhyme. Her sentences have a logic all their own, just as she has a logic of her own. She says of herself that she prefers to be called Ada rather than Adah, as Ada is a perfect palindrome — it can read either forward or backward, just as she can. She often reads books from front to back, then back to front. And the Congo she says is a fine place to read the same book many times. She identifies with language. It is a living, vital being to her.

"LANGUAGE CAN BE USED AS A FORM OF COERCION AND PUNISHMENT."

Nathan uses language in the exact opposite way as Adah. For him, language is static, and words are perfectly uniform in meaning. Language can be used as punishment. Words have one meaning, and he knows what that meaning is. He wishes to impose the word of God on the Congo as he has imposed it on his family. Nathan's use of "the Verse" as a form of punishment for the girls is especially telling. When they misbehave in any way, he has the perfect verse to show them their error and correct them. They must mechanically write out these words as a punishment and a correction. It does serve as a punishment, but none of the girls seems to gain any knowledge or wisdom from it. They understand this exercise as a form of torture, not education, and they come to despise Nathan for it. This situation is yet another instance of Nathan's blindness and stubbornness. His use of words makes his children hate him and may also make them mistrust the very book he wants them to value and love. He turns the Bible into poison.

○ ○ ◯

What does Kingsolver say about the role of women in society?

"KINGSOLVER USES THE 1950s TO EXPLORE HOW WOMEN'S LIVES HAVE CHANGED SINCE."

At the beginning of the novel, it's Rachel, the beauty, who best exemplifies our stereotype of the role of women in the late 1950s in the South. In that time and in that society, women were raised to be lovely objects, not to think, not to be educated—certainly not to question their fathers or husbands. Nathan makes it clear that sending girls to college is a complete waste of time, money, and effort. Even the sensible and self-respecting Leah is afraid no one will want to marry her just because she's a whiz in school. Orleanna, encouraging her girls to sew and embroider for their hope chests, continues to believe that finding the right man and marrying is the only path for a young girl. She believes this despite her own unhappy experience as handmaiden to Nathan.

But Adah, who never marries, comes home to attend college and medical school, then takes on a challenging career in research science. This would have been almost unthinkable in the 1950s but is possible in the later decades when she undertakes this path. Still, the possibility of combining family life and a difficult career eludes her—and perhaps it's still difficult in this country. It's not impossible, but it remains hard for a woman to have both a career and a family in twenty-first century America.

By the end of the novel, perceptions of the roles of women change for the Price girls. Only Rachel, who remains in white South Africa, where time is frozen in the 1950s, stays wedded to the old values of the American South. Leah, always a tomboy, learns to shoot, participates in a hunt, teaches in school, and later has positions of responsibility in her society. She marries a black African and creates with him a marriage of mutual respect and equality. Adah not only goes to college, but continues on to medical school. She pursues a challenging career in research science, a field that has long been restricted to men. Still, the possibility of combining family life and a difficult career eludes Adah.

"IN THE CONGO, THE ROLE OF WOMEN IS CONTINUAL WORK."

At one point in the novel, Kingsolver writes, "While the little boys ran around pretending to shoot each other and fall dead in the road, it appeared that little girls were running the country." Men in the Congo are allowed to have more than one wife. The richer and more powerful the man, the more wives he can support. The women work all the time, literally wearing their bodies out. They begin bearing children when they're still children themselves. And they mourn their children, who die with alarming frequency, alone. They can't attend school even for the short time that the boys do. They're subject to ritual circumcision, a rite that requires the excision of the clitoris, which leaves women without genital feeling or the ability to experience sexual pleasure. It also often causes them permanent physical damage and pain. The mere fact that Leah teaches in school along with Anatole causes a scandal. Later, she's not allowed to hunt with the men until a vote is taken. And Leah's participation in the hunt becomes a sore spot, which indirectly leads to the great tragedy of the novel, the death of Ruth May.

○ ○ ○

What does the title mean?

"THE TITLE IS A RIDDLE THAT THE NOVEL SOLVES."

The title is initially a riddle. How can these two opposites go together? How can the seemingly sacred Bible be poison? The novel takes these two opposites and makes them go together. Nathan's Bible, his rigid interpretation of the sacred text in a society that has its own sacred texts and teachings, is poison. The people of the Congo learn to stay away from it, just as he learns to stay away from the burning poisonwood plant. The Bible, which is supposed to bring healing to those who read it, brings only trouble to the Congo. Likewise, the missionaries who try to impose their Bible, their beliefs, and their customs on the Africans wind up causing pain. Understanding the link the title creates is crucial to understanding Kingsolver's message in the novel.

"THE DOUBLE MEANING OF 'POISONWOOD' ILLUMINATES NATHAN'S CHARACTER AND POSITION IN THE VILLAGE."

Bangala means "precious" as well as "powerful," "dangerous," and "poison-wood," depending on how it's pronounced. Over the course of the novel, Kingsolver shows the Bible to be all of these things. It's precious and powerful to Nathan, and he wishes it to be the same for his family and for his congregation. Unfortunately, he doesn't understand the other meanings of *bangala*, so he fails to notice that his Bible and its teachings are dangerous to the people. He himself mispronounces the word, unknowingly calling the Bible "poisonwood" when he means to call it "precious." "Tata Jesus is *Bangala*," Nathan declares at the end of his sermons. He means to say that Jesus is precious and dear, but instead pronounces the word so that it means the poisonwood tree. Jesus, Nathan effectively says, will make you itch like the devil. It's Adah who points this out with malicious glee. The congregation, ready to mock their ineffectual preacher, notices the error as well. Nathan and his gospel become a source of ridicule and contempt. The poisonwood gospel that Nathan preaches is a mistake from the smallest matters of pronunciation to the largest matters of faith. In this way, the title *The Poisonwood Bible* turns out to be a cruel joke.

Like language in general, the Bible can be used in many ways, some healing, some harmful. Language, like the Bible, has many interpretations, misinterpretations, and mistranslations. When Brother Fowles visits and is asked whether the Bible is God's word, he explains, "God's word, brought to you by a crew of romantic idealists in a harsh desert culture eons ago, followed by a chain of translators two thousand years long." Leah is confused by this idea but willing to consider it. Nathan, on the other hand, says he's never been troubled by difficulties when interpreting God's word. But Brother Fowles says that he has heard many mistranslations of the Bible, even many comical ones. Nathan's own comical mistranslation of *bangala* escapes him, as does the deeper meaning of his conversation with Brother Fowles. Nathan believes that he is and must be right. The possibility of multiple translations and multiple meanings is impossible for him. He must have the one right answer. So *The Poisonwood Bible* comes to carry one possible meaning—the rigid reading of the Bible according to Nathan Price.

○ ○ ○

Why is the novel told from the points of view of five women?

"THIS STRUCTURE GIVES VOICE TO WOMEN WHO TRADITIONALLY HAVE NONE."

At the time the novel takes place, women in the American South and in Africa traditionally had no voices. But in the novel itself, women are the only ones who *do* have voices. The story, as it unfolds through the voices of women, is personal, and the personal reflects the political. The Price women see the world in personal terms but nonetheless convey the larger political meanings, and convey them with powerful emotional force. Powerfully, Nathan's voice is absent from the narrative. We hear him clearly enough, but always through the women. Though we hear it second-hand, his voice is booming. We also hear Anatole only indirectly. It's mostly through Leah that we learn about who Anatole is and what he fights for. His voice also is noticeably missing. These strong men must speak through their women.

"THE FIVE DIFFERENT WAYS OF SEEING AND EXPERIENCING ARE COMPLEMENTARY."

Each of the Price women sees the world very differently. Each voice presents the experience of the Congo in a distinct way, and all the voices together make up a coherent whole. When we first hear about an event from one point of view, we're inclined to accept that account as true—but then the second voice comes to alter or expand our impression. Then the third adds more, the fourth even more. Leah offers a sensible, often idealistic view, but then Rachel often undercuts this view with her own self-centered and limited vision—which Adah in turn comments on slyly and astutely. Ruth May is relatively free, able to express the prejudice and innocence of an unselfconscious child.

Through this structure we learn how to read each character, how to correct for her faults in vision. We learn quickly to discount Rachel as beauty-obsessed, silly, and selfish. Similarly, we come to understand that Ruth May doesn't always grasp the weight of what she's saying. Adah takes longer to understand, as she applies her singular vision to the world of language and meaning. As an outsider who thinks of herself as different—lame and mute—she comments on the action but takes little part in it. And Leah grows from idealistically loyal, uncritical of her father and his beliefs, to a woman of mature and independent judgment. Her voice undergoes the greatest change. Altogether, the voices comment on one another, so that the meaning gleaned from all the voices is much greater than that obtained from the individual parts. Reality seeps in through the cracks between the characters' different voices.

"THE USE OF FIVE VOICES SUGGESTS THAT NO SINGLE VOICE HAS THE TRUTH."

The five different voices each convey only a partial truth. Taken together, they convey a more complete truth—but they also suggest that there is no absolute truth. Historical accuracy depends on the idea that we can know the truth, that we can know what happened. The five voices here make it clear that no one person ever knows the whole truth, and that even five people together can't know it. The history of a single family, like the much more complicated history of the Congo, is full of mystery, mistake, and misunderstanding. We don't really know what happened in the Congo, why independence failed, why Lumumba was killed with the help of the CIA, why Mobutu maintained power for so long. We can try to answer these and similar historical questions—but only provisionally. We can never know the complete truth.

○ ○ ○

Why does the novel begin where it does, with Orleanna in Sanderling Island long after the events in the Congo?

"ORLEANNA'S VOICE AT THE START OF THE NOVEL PREPARES US FOR TRAGEDY."

From the mournful tone of the beginning, we're prepared for tragedy, for terrible events. On the first page, Orleanna refers to her girls as "pale, doomed blossoms." She refers to herself as the mother of children living and dead. These ominous words prepare us to see a child die. We don't know which one or how, but we know that at least one of Orleanna's children will die. She also says in her opening lamentation, "I trod on Africa without a thought, straight from our family's divinely inspired beginning to our terrible end." We can't understand the full meaning of this statement when we first read it, but it carries a heavy weight. In this way, the beginning sets the tone and themes of mourning, guilt, and responsibility that run through the entire novel.

"THE BEGINNING CREATES SUSPENSE."

From the start, we know terrible things are going to happen. Orleanna prepares us for the death of a child and for her own horrible mistakes. Her opening remarks are filled with guilt and remorse for her own arrogance and blindness, for going into Africa without knowing what she was doing in any way. She's overwhelmed by her own sense of responsibility for what happened. Over and over again in the opening pages, she confesses to her own ignorance, to her own complicity. She is all conscience. Such a heavy burden of guilt makes us fear the worst—what can Orleanna have done to merit so much misery and self-punishment? We read on to discover, if we dare.

"THE BEGINNING CREATES A STRONG IDENTIFICATION WITH AND FEELING FOR ORLEANNA."

The great blame and responsibility we see Orleanna take on at the opening of the novel renders us sympathetic toward her. We don't know what she has done, but we're ready to forgive her because we see the depth of her remorse. We even tend to think she's being too hard on herself. In this way, the beginning creates a strong bond between us and Orleanna. This character comes across as believable and trustworthy. Orleanna portrays herself and her situation in the worst possible terms. Orleanna doesn't plead her case, doesn't ask for leniency, and doesn't explain away her role with accounts of extenuating circumstances. We have confidence that she'll tell her story honestly.

○ ○ ○

Why does the novel end where it does?

"ORLEANNA FINDS FORGIVENESS."

The final line, "Move on. Walk forward into the light," gives Orleanna the permission she asked for in the very beginning of the novel—to forgive herself, to let go of her guilt and leave the past behind. These words are hopeful about the future and generous about the past. Orleanna's guilt over her inaction, her complicity, her participation in the tragedy of her family finally lifts with this line. The novel thus ends in forgiveness and optimism about the future for Orleanna and, by extension, for the Congo. We sense that there will be a better future for Orleanna and for Africa. Kingsolver provides a moving and optimistic ending to a story that is at times grim.

"A MYSTERIOUS NEW VOICE GRANTS CLOSURE."

The ending of the novel is told in a strange new voice. It's a voice we haven't heard before, and it's mystifying, even a bit confusing. Where are we? Who's talking to us? "I am *muntu*, Africa, *muntu* one child and a million all lost on the same day." The voice announces itself as Africa and as Ruth May. As Ruth May, the voice is the voice of the dead. "Being dead is not worse than being alive. It is different, though. You could say the view is larger." So this is the larger view, the historical view, the ghostly view. This disembodied voice and ghostly tone pull up and away from the actual story and lift the novel to another, higher plane. The work ends in a new place in which it comments on itself and places itself within history. It's a long and lovely view, as if Kingsolver were hovering above her own creation and sealing it shut.

"KILANGA HAS DISAPPEARED FROM MAPS AND FROM MEMORY."

By the end of the novel, the village of Kilanga has disappeared not only from the map but also from memory. No one remembers that there ever was such a village. The Price family past is erased from Africa. In the larger picture, the events of the novel didn't happen—they don't matter. Africa moves on. Children die and parents grieve and history continues. This is a view from a distance, which provides forgiveness for Orleanna. What she did or didn't do has faded from the world's sight. And it should fade from her memory. History moves forward, just as Orleanna should. Although this disappearance seems sad at first, ultimately it isn't. It doesn't mean that the Price story had no meaning or consequence. Obviously it did. But it does mean that the Price story has no ultimate consequences. History has swallowed it up and moved on.

$$\circ \quad \circ \quad \circ$$

Is the ending of the novel satisfying?

"YES, THE CHARACTERS FOLLOW THE PATHS THEY'VE FOLLOWED FROM THE START."

The characters each follow a path that leads to his or her proper end. Leah, always idealistic and brave, ends up happily married to a man who loves her and whose cause she can fight for. She bears children who will continue in the fight. She has always wanted this, and she deserves to get it. That her husband is a black African attests to the degree to which she's left the American South behind. Rachel, like Leah, ends just where she should, successfully taking care of herself. She has always been the survivor, the one who knows how to get what she needs. By the novel's close, she gets a hotel to run. The racist situation in South Africa doesn't bother her at all—it's not even clear if she knows of the government policy that keeps blacks and whites separate. In fact, Rachel seems perfectly comfortable running her all-white hotel.

Adah's end is in many ways the most satisfying. She heals herself, educates herself, and finds important work to do that will be of help to Africa. The beginning of the novel finds her silent, an outsider and observer, but she eventually is engaged with life. Ruth May's family's sacrifices her to Africa. Her death is in no way just or correct—but it is necessary. Orleanna forgives herself in the end, and this is a triumph. Nathan, on the other hand, ends the novel mad and alone. Though to some extent he's always been so, the end of the novel amplifies his condition to its full, unfortunate expression.

"YES, THE ENDING IS FITTING BUT NOT NECESSARILY JUST."

Yes, the characters end where their paths were leading them, but the ending isn't completely fair. The truly good characters suffer greatly while the evil ones don't suffer enough. Although Leah marries, has children, and leads a full and productive life, she struggles against constant hardship and terror. She deserves a more tranquil happiness. The foolish, vain, and selfish Rachel ends with more than she deserves. She should at least have a little self-knowledge, a little self-consciousness. In the end she claims not to understand why her family doesn't visit her, indicating that she still lacks even the remotest idea about the world and her place in it. Adah has the most satisfying end. She deserves happiness and she finds it in work. She never seems destined for romantic or family happiness. Orleanna deserves far more. She forgives herself, but not until long after the events, long after years of guilt, remorse, regret. She deserves to feel better sooner. And Nathan deserves to be punished more horribly than he is. Like Rachel, he never achieves self-consciousness, never understands what he did to his family, and never takes responsibility for it.

"NO, THE ENDING IS UNSATISFYING BECAUSE KINGSOLVER DOESN'T REVEAL NATHAN'S FATE."

The most unsatisfying part of the ending is the lack of hard knowledge about Nathan's fate. We never really learn what happens to him—whether he suffers, whether he undergoes some conversion into madness, or dies. We don't know his response to the death of Ruth May or his reaction to his family's abandonment of him. In many ways, Nathan is the weakest, most one-dimensional character in the novel, and his end is similarly weak. We suspect he goes mad. We picture him solitary and raving in the African jungle. But what are the particulars of his madness? We want to know whether he ever learns anything from his experience, whether he repents, grieves, feels remorse or responsibility. Kingsolver seems to lose interest in him and his story.

Proudly Political

Unlike many contemporary authors, Kingsolver maintains an unwavering political voice.

○ ○ ○

BARBARA KINGSOLVER IS A POLITICAL WRITER, one who imbeds in each novel a socioeconomic theme—a cause. There are few other such American novelists who either identify as or can be labeled political. But Kingsolver is steadfast in this identity. She is a fierce advocate and supporter of other writers committed to social change. Her life, like her novels, is marked by her commitment to social justice. She has woven her life and her politics together, living what she believes in, believing in how she lives.

It's not surprising to learn that Kingsolver was raised in a politically active household. In the introductory note to *The Poisonwood Bible*, she says of her upbringing: "I was the fortunate child of medical and public-health workers, whose compassion and curiosity led them to the Congo. They brought me to a place of wonders, taught me to pay attention, and set me early on a path of exploring the great, shifting terrain between righteousness and what's right." Kingsolver's father, a physician in a poor rural Kentucky town, was admired and respected for treating the poor, often for free. Barbara, born in 1955, grew up learning from these socially aware and intellectually curious parents. Her mother was a great reader, encouraging her to explore books and the local library. It was there that Kingsolver discovered books that changed her life, especially the novels of George Eliot and, later, Doris Lessing.

Kingsolver was acutely aware of the vast social and economic disparity between rich and poor, white and black, in Kentucky. Although her own family was decidedly middle-class, she identified with the area's uneducated, economically depressed farmers and other residents. She was a shy child who was unusually tall for her age. Self-conscious and different, young Kingsolver was an outsider. Traveling with her adventurous parents to distant places accentuated this feeling of being an outsider. With her parents, Kingsolver traveled to the Caribbean, where her father worked in a convent hospital. At the age of seven, she spent close to a year in central Africa.

Despite a love for the landscape of rural Kentucky and an admiration for her committed parents, Kingsolver left her home state to attend DePauw University in Indiana on a music scholarship. Always interested in the natural world, she studied anatomy and physiology and majored in biology. Her love of books and her early attempts at poetry and fiction led her to minor in English. At college during the 1970s, she joined in political activism of many kinds—protesting the war in Vietnam, abortion laws, racism, sexism. She read Karl Marx and Betty Friedan. At nineteen, Kingsolver was the victim of date rape, at the time an unnamed and unprosecutable offense. After graduating *magna cum laude* in 1977, she traveled in Europe, working at odd jobs to support herself.

Upon returning to the United States, Kingsolver enrolled in the University of Arizona in Tucson and received a master's degree in 1981. She remained in Tucson, writing scientific articles for the university and beginning to write freelance journalistic pieces on the political issues that had always consumed her. Finally, her writing and her activism began to come together. Her reporting on the strike against the Phelps Dodge copper mining company in southern Arizona in 1983 eventually became the article "Holding the Line," which established her as a professional journalist.

Waiting for change

"I am horribly out-of-fashion. I want to change the world. I write because I have a passion for storytelling, but also because I believe fiction is an extraordinary tool for creating empathy and compassion." —Barbara Kingsolver from R. Matuz, *Contemporary Literary Criticism Yearbook*, 1988

In 1985, Kingsolver married Joseph Hoffman and had a daughter, Camille, in 1987. In 1992, however, the marriage dissolved. Then, on a writing fellowship in Virginia in 1993, she met ornithologist and animal behaviorist Steven Hopp, who became her second husband in 1995. Together, they have a daughter, Lily.

> What separates Kingsolver from other novelists is that she is an activist first and a novelist second.

Kingsolver has led an unusual life for a novelist. Having studied literature and writing less extensively than many other novelists, she is largely self-taught. Her political activism, which has figured deeply in her personal and professional choices, has also directed her fiction writing. She writes about causes that matter to her, and she writes about them with deep conviction.

Her first novel, *The Bean Trees* (1988), explores the lives of marginally poor, single mothers and children in rural Kentucky. After the success of this first novel, *Holding the Line: Women in the Great Arizona Mine Strike of 1983* was published in 1989. *Homeland and Other Stories* came out in 1989 and was named an American Library Association notable book the following year. *Animal Dreams* (1990) focuses on Native Americans as well as on environmental issues, parental relationships, women's issues, and the U.S. involvement in Nicaragua. It was awarded the PEN fiction prize.

In 1992, Kingsolver published a collection of poetry, *Another America / Otra America*, written in both English and Spanish. *Pigs in Heaven*, her next novel, returned to characters who first appeared in *Animal Dreams* and continued to explore issues surrounding the plight of Native Americans. *High Tide in Tucson: Essays from Now or Never* (1995) reprinted a selection of Kingsolver's journalistic pieces.

The Poisonwood Bible (1998) was recognized immediately as a departure for Kingsolver. Critics hailed it as a stunning leap forward, both in narrative complexity and in the scope of its political, social and cultural concerns. Kingsolver followed up with *Prodigal Summer* (2000), which, while well received, didn't live up to the high standards set by *The Poisonwood Bible*.

What separates Kingsolver from other novelists is that she is an activist first and a novelist second. Her novels are, for her, a way of communicating her commitment to social and economic justice. She has consistently written on issues of ecology, feminism, Central and South America, and Native Americans and their cultures. With *The Poisonwood Bible*, Kingsolver explored the effects of colonialism on the native peoples of Africa.

Kingsolver is forthright about her desire to use fiction to uncover truth. In *High Tide in Tucson*, she writes, "What seems right to me . . . is to represent the world I can see and touch as honestly as I know how, and when writing fiction, to use that variegated world as a matrix for the characters and conflicts I need to fathom. This moral and political high-mindedness goes along with a desire for wide accessibility: "I want to write books that anybody can read. . . . I want to challenge people who like literature, to give them something for their trouble, without closing any doors to people who are less educated." Such attitudes are rare for novelists. Many writers claim to be unconcerned with their audience and insist their art trumps any political agenda. Kingsolver is up front about her intent: she has causes she cares about deeply, and she uses her writing to raise awareness of them.

A Wounded Land

The tumultuous sweep of Congolese history that runs beneath the novel mirrors the personal trials of the Price family.

○ ○ ○

THE CONGO FIGURES in *The Poisonwood Bible* as far more than a setting—it's integral to the novel itself. As Kingsolver says in her author's note, "The historical figures and events described here are as real as I could render them with the help of recorded history, in all its fascinating variations." At the end of the novel, she provides a two-page bibliography that includes many major historical works. The integrity of Kingsolver's attempt to do justice to the Congo's history would be difficult to refute.

The early history of the Congo, which Kingsolver refers to only in fragments, is testament to European greed, exploitation, and violence. In 1881, following the explorations of Anglo-American explorer Henry M. Stanley, King Leopold II of Belgium created a trading post and settlement in Leopoldville with international financial backing. In 1885, the General Act of Berlin recognized Leopold as the sovereign of the new state of the Congo. Through ruthless suppression of opposition and the exploitation of African labor, Leopold held his grasp on the Congo and continued to reap huge profits from its bountiful resources.

The one historical event that actually occurs during the timeframe of *The Poisonwood Bible*—the inauguration of Patrice Lumumba on June 30, 1960—is reported by Leah, who is uncertain of what she is seeing and who can't understand the language being used. Still, Leah is impressed by Lumumba's stature and moved by the crowd's enthusiastic response to him. The *New York Times* of July 1, 1960, reports this event with the headline "Lumumba Assails Colonialism as Congo Is Freed" and begins with this sentence: "An attack on colonialism by the Premier of the new Republic of Congo marred the ceremonies today in which King Baudouin of the Belgians proclaimed the territory's independence. . . . [The event] was abruptly transformed by the militant speech of Premier Patrice Lumumba, who cited the sufferings of the African people at the hands of the whites." The *New York Times* clearly had its own priorities and point of view at the time, which can be factored in among the many other points of view we hear in the novel. In its sympathies, the *Times* seems closer to Nathan Price and Eeben Axelroot than to Leah or Anatole.

The other political events related in the novel all conform to the historical record. There are the atrocities committed against African workers in the mines, the systematic exploitation of the riches of Africa, the plots to undermine and overthrow Lumumba, the attempted secession of Katanga province, the CIA-assisted murder of Lumumba, the violence in the Congo following independence, the flight of most Europeans, the return of the outsiders to "restore order," the molestation of American missionaries, and the installation of Mobutu. In the 1950s and 1960s, Congo became known for postcolonial chaos and savagery. It also became black Africa's first Cold War battleground. Orleanna keeps a picture of President Eisenhower tacked to the wall of the cooking house. She is unaware of his participation in the bloody events in Africa and is uncritical of his role in the Congo. He is her president, and she supports him blindly, just as she supports her husband.

The actual historical events in the Congo unfolded in dramatic sequence. Patrice Lumumba and Joseph Kasavubu shared power for a period of one week in May 1960. When army units mutinied, nearly all Europeans left the country. At the time that the fictional Nathan Price was preparing his Easter sermon (to be delivered on July 4, 1960), the Congo declared its independence on June 30. When the government ran into trouble soon after, it asked the United Nations for help. In July 1960, Katanga province, the richest part of the Congo, declared itself an independent country. U.N. troops began to arrive on July 15, 1960, and remained until 1964.

On September 5, 1960, President Kasavubu dismissed Patrice Lumumba. Joseph Mobutu, an army colonel, set up a provisional government at Leopoldville (now known as Kinshasa). Lumumba was imprisoned. His loyal followers established a rival government at Stanleyville (now known as Kisangani), under the leadership of Antoine Gizenga. Quickly, other provinces declared their independence, so that by November 1960, there were four separate governments in the Congo. In January 1961, the popular Lumumba, who may well have been able to unite the country, was assassinated in Katanga with help from the CIA and the other branches of the U.S. government.

While these political events provide a backdrop to the events of *The Poisonwood Bible*, life in Kilanga goes on as before. The Price family continues in its struggles, as do the native villagers. Politics does not intrude on them directly.

Anatole's long and tireless opposition to Mobutu, his fears for himself and his family, his many brutal imprisonments, also coincide with the historical facts. Despite rebel invasions of Katanga in 1977 and 1978, Mobutu maintained his rule. Belgian, French and Moroccan troops, many ferried in by U.S. planes, rescued Mobutu from rebel forces. Mobutu thus came to rely heavily on the West for his survival and also became an indispensable asset to the West. The CIA used an airstrip in the remote Shaban town of Kamina for covert transfer of weapons to neighboring Angola, making it a strategic outpost for the Reagan Doctrine. President Reagan spoke of Mobutu as "A voice of good sense and good will." Mobutu held power in the Congo for thirty-five long years. But by the end of *The Poisonwood Bible*, he runs away in the dark. For the Congo, this departure is the beginning of light.

An Ever Bigger Canvas

The Poisonwood Bible both remains true to the themes of Kingsolver's earlier novels and expands her horizons considerably.

○　○　○

AT FIRST GLANCE, *The Poisonwood Bible* seems like a big departure for Kingsolver. Having built a reputation on three novels set in the southwestern United States, she suddenly makes a round-the-world jump to the jungles of Africa. Despite the globetrotting, *The Poisonwood Bible* isn't as drastic a change as it seems. Kingsolver's first three novels—*The Bean Trees*, *Pigs in Heaven*, and *Animal Dreams*—investigate the relationships between the political, spiritual, and social spheres, just as *The Poisonwood Bible* docs. All four novels explore these relationships through complex characters and predicaments.

What's different about *The Poisonwood Bible* is that it's the first time Kingsolver has taken on these issues on such a grand scale. As Sarah Kerr noted in the *New York Times*, "Where [Kingsolver's] earlier books tended to be simple and sweet, the new one is learned, tragicomic and sprawling. It is also more truly the work of an activist—critical, especially, of American involvement in the assassination of Prime Minister Patrice Lumumba and the installation of the dictator Mobutu." In short, Kingsolver decided to think big, and it paid off.

Like a number of major recent novels, *The Poisonwood Bible* drew its share of controversy. A year and a half before its publication, there was some commotion when it was reported that Kingsolver was unhappy with some of the authors—Newt Gingrich, among others—that her longtime publisher, HarperCollins, represented. *Publishers Weekly* reported that

Kingsolver, as part of her contract, wanted HarperCollins to establish the Bellwether Prize for Fiction recognizing "literature of social change." She would fund the $25,000 prize, while HarperCollins would guarantee a first printing of 10,000 copies of the winning novel. Indeed, Kingsolver did eventually fund the prize and ultimately remained with HarperCollins.

Upon its publication in 1998, *The Poisonwood Bible* was named an ABBY (American Booksellers Book of the Year) honor book, won the Patterson Fiction Prize, and was short-listed for the Orange Prize. The *New York Times*, the *Los Angeles Times*, and the *Village Voice* all named it one of the best books of 1998. In perhaps the most lucrative of these honors, Kingsolver's work appeared as a selection on Oprah's Book Club in the summer of 2000. Oprah described *The Poisonwood Bible* as "a suspenseful epic of one family's tragic undoing and remarkable reconstruction," a novel of "passionately intertwined stories [that] become a compelling exploration of moral risk and personal responsibility."

Reviews in virtually every media outlet made similar proclamations, praising Kingsolver for her willingness to tackle a large and difficult subject and for her success in creating a moving human drama. Verlyn Klinkenborg of the *New York Times Book Review* wrote, "The Congo permeates *The Poisonwood Bible*, and yet this is a novel that is just as much about America, a portrait, in absentia, of the nation that sent the Prices to save the souls of a people for whom it felt only contempt . . ." Sarah Kerr continued in this vein in a piece in the *New York Times*: "There's a majesty, a nineteenth-century-novel echo to this sweeping vision of nature doing its thing independent of the human will. It's an effect that perhaps only Kingsolver, of all contemporary novelists, has the expertise to pull off."

Even better than the real thing

"There are little things that people who know me might recognize in my novels. But my work is not about me. I don't ever write about real people. That would be stealing, first of all. And second of all, art is supposed to be better than that. If you want a slice of life, look out the window. An artist has to look out that window, isolate one or two suggestive things, and embroider them together with poetry and fabrication, to create a revelation."
—Barbara Kingsolver, Authors on the Web

Perhaps the most enthusiastic review comes from John Leonard in *The Nation*: "Kingsolver has dreamed a magnificent fiction and a ferocious bill of indictment. . . . In case I haven't made myself clear, what we have here—with this new, mature, angry, heartbroken, expansive out-of-Africa Kingsolver—is at last our very own [Doris] Lessing and our very own [Nadine] Gordimer."

Hillary Clinton became the novel's most famous praise-giver when she reported in *O: The Oprah Magazine* that she found *The Poisonwood Bible* "one of the most powerful books I've read about the evil consequences of patriarchal oppression, be it personal, cultural or political."

Kingsolver won effusive praise not only from reviewers but from her fellow authors as well. Novelist Jane Smiley called *The Poisonwood Bible* "ambitious, successful and beautiful." She went on, "This awed reviewer hardly knows where to begin. . . . It is fascinating sentence by sentence; the sentences add up to unexpected and compelling scenes; the scenes make a whole world out of one that is alien to most of us."

Smiley did, however, perceive one serious flaw in the novel—the character of Nathan Price: "Nathan's one-sidedness reflects our culture's failure to understand the humanity of those who seem to be the source of evil. . . . As a character, he never comes alive. He is cause and effect, but never a man. . . . Kingsolver's ideological slip shows, and the imperfection persists to the end of the novel. The author loses interest in Nathan, tries to compensate by giving him a dramatic death that seems pale in the telling. This failure goes right to the heart of who we are as a culture and how we look at ourselves."

Another critique came from Michiko Kakutani of the *New York Times*. "Efforts by Ms. Kingsolver to turn the story of the Price family into a social allegory can be heavy-handed at times, transforming many of her characters into one-dimensional pawns in a starkly lighted morality play." But Kakutani goes on to say, "One of the things that keeps *The Poisonwood Bible* from becoming overly schematic and lends the novel a fierce emotional undertow is Ms. Kingsolver's love of detail, her eye for the small facts of daily life..." and concludes, "[T]he reader is made to understand not only the ways in which a father's sins are visited upon (and expiated by) his children, but also the ways in which private lives can be shaped and shattered by public events."

The Poisonwood Bible

With such sweeping acclaim and phenomenal sales, *The Poisonwood Bible* stands as Kingsolver's most important novel to date. In 2000, Kingsolver followed up with *Prodigal Summer*—but, as Jennifer Schuessler of the *New York Times* wrote, "Readers hoping for the emotional intensity and wide-angle vision of *The Poisonwood Bible,* Kingsolver's magnificent 1998 epic . . . will most likely be disappointed." Though this latest effort was by no means panned, critics overwhelmingly agreed that *The Poisonwood Bible* remains Kingsolver's finest achievement to date.

Other Books of Interest

The Poisonwood Bible builds on both Kingsolver's own earlier novels and the works of other great postcolonial writers.

○ ○ ○

BY BARBARA KINGSOLVER

THE BEAN TREES
    (Harper & Row, 1988)
Kingsolver's first novel focuses on a group of strong-willed and mutually supportive women in Kentucky. An abandoned Cherokee child forms the center of a nontraditional family of women.

ANIMAL DREAMS
    (HarperCollins, 1990)
Bigotry, disease, pollution and the political brutalities in Central America all figure prominently in *Animal Dreams*. The heroine, hoping to find stability and peace after the rat race of urban life, instead finds only difficulties.

PIGS IN HEAVEN
    (HarperCollins, 1993)
A sequel to *The Bean Trees*, this novel traces the legal problems of adopting the Cherokee child introduced in that earlier novel. Kingsolver brings issues of cultural and ethnic heritage and identity to the forefront of this political and somewhat sentimental work.

PRODIGAL SUMMER
(HarperCollins, 2000)
Kingsolver's most recent novel returns to the turf (the American Southwest) of her earlier novels and focuses on a new one (sex). Like her other novels, it features plucky women, liberal politics and a vibrant appreciation of the natural world.

BY OTHER AUTHORS

A GUEST OF HONOUR (Viking, 1970); **THE CONSERVATIONIST** (Viking, 1975); **BURGER'S DAUGHTER** (Viking, 1979); **JULY'S PEOPLE** (Viking, 1989); **A SPORT OF NATURE** (Knopf, 1987); **THE HOUSE GUN** (Farrar, Straus & Giroux, 1998)
by Nadine Gordimer
The South African–born Gordimer is renowned for her provocative writing about her experiences and imaginings of her native country. She's the contemporary novelist who most closely resembles Kingsolver (the two are often compared). Gordimer's novels, all of which are set in South Africa, treat questions of race and gender sensitively and sympathetically, exploring the problems of whites and blacks living together.

THE GOLDEN NOTEBOOK (1962); **THE CHILDREN OF VIOLENCE NOVELS** (1952–1959)
by Doris Lessing
Kingsolver has identified Lessing as one of her foremost influences. Indeed, generations of women and women writers have gained inspiration from Lessing and her unique, early feminist vision.
The Golden Notebook, which focuses on a woman's life in man's world, is the most renowned of Lessing's works and also the one most closely related to Kingsolver's. One section of the novel, "The Black Notebook," records the heroine's youthful experiences in colonial Africa, connecting *The Golden Notebook* to *The Poisonwood Bible* in both its geographic setting and its feminist content.
Of Lessing's five-novel *Children of Violence* cycle, Kingsolver said, "I read [these] novels and began to understand how a person could write about the problems of the world in a compelling and beautiful way. And

it seemed to me that was the most important thing I could ever do, if I could ever do that."

THINGS FALL APART
(Heinemann, 1959)
by Chinua Achebe

Acclaimed as perhaps the greatest work of fiction to emerge from twentieth-century Africa, *Things Fall Apart* is a story of missionary Christianity, social change, and racism set in an African village during the 1880s. Kingsolver has cited the novel as influential on her research and writing of *The Poisonwood Bible*. Much like Kingsolver four decades later, Achebe simultaneously reveals character and reflects on political and social change.

HEART OF DARKNESS
(1902)
by Joseph Conrad

This classic short novel is the definitive story of Europeans in Africa, the novel that most forcefully presents the European colonialist view of the "dark continent" and its perils. Conrad's story of Kurtz, an Englishman who loses his way in Africa, and the expedition sent to locate him, inspired Francis Ford Coppola's acclaimed 1979 film *Apocalypse Now*. In *The Poisonwood Bible*, Kingsolver's final vision of Nathan Price alone and mad somewhere in the wildness of the Congo bears a striking, and not unintentional, resemblance to Conrad's portrait of Kurtz.